A Nose for Trouble

Other Avon Camelot Books by
Nancy Hope Wilson

BRINGING NETTIE BACK

NANCY HOPE WILSON was born in Boston and grew up in suburban Massachusetts and rural Vermont. She is a graduate of Swarthmore College and the Harvard Graduate School of Education, and she has taught in day-care centers, elementary schools, high schools, nursing homes, and human service agencies. She also worked for five years as a carpenter. Her other books include two novels, *Bringing Nettie Back* and *The Reason for Janey,* and a picture book, *Helen and the Hudson Hornet.* She lives in Amherst, Massachusetts, with her husband and two children.

A Nose for Trouble

NANCY HOPE WILSON

Illustrated by Doron Ben-Ami

AN AVON CAMELOT BOOK

A NOSE FOR TROUBLE is an original publication of Avon Books. This work has never before appeared in book form. Any similarity to actual persons or events is purely coincidental.

AVON BOOKS
A division of
The Hearst Corporation
1350 Avenue of the Americas
New York, New York 10019

Copyright © 1994 by Nancy Hope Wilson
Illustrations by Doron Ben-Ami
Illustrations © 1994 by Avon Books
Published by arrangement with the author
Library of Congress Catalog Card Number: 94-94465
ISBN: 0-380-77344-9
RL: 2.6

First Avon Camelot Printing: November 1994

CAMELOT TRADEMARK REG. U.S. PAT. OFF. AND IN OTHER COUNTRIES, MARCA REGISTRADA, HECHO EN U.S.A.

Printed in the U.S.A.

OPM   10 9 8 7 6 5 4 3 2 1

To my five siblings:
T., Nora, Rod, Dawes, Patricia.
Hurray for all the differences!

Acknowledgments

I am very grateful for the generosity and enthusiasm of Carmen Calinda Brown and her mother, Lois Brown; of Scooter Case and his father, David Case; and of Mike Legare. From some I learned about using a wheelchair; from all I gained insight into how a disability affects daily life.

I am also indebted to Paul Petruski, electrician; to David Dion, firefighter; and to Dr. Stephen Hickman, pediatrician. Each contributed invaluable expertise to the development of this story.

I thank my writers' group for their discerning critique of the manuscript, and especially Cynthia Stowe for her particular involvement and encouragement.

Chapter 1

"We could come with you," Mom said. "Just this first day," Dad added.

I smiled at them. I knew they were nervous. So was I. But no other fifth-grader would bring her parents on the first day of school.

"Thanks," I said, "but I'm already different enough!"

They both laughed, which made me laugh, too.

"You're different, all right," Mom said. She leaned over my wheelchair to give me a hug. "There's no one quite like our Maggie May Mitzkovitz!"

Dad hugged me, too. *"Vive la différence!"*

he cheered. He says that a lot. It's French for ''Hurray for the difference.''

When the special bus came, my little brother, Howie, climbed into my lap.

''Veeva lahdee French!'' he said.

He gave me a big kiss that smelled of milk and banana. Everybody tells me I've got a very sensitive nose. It's a problem sometimes. Once in my old school, there was a nasty, sour sponge in the kitchen. I got whiffs of it no matter where I sat in the lunchroom. Everybody thought I was crazy till one day the custodian moved the fridge and found the moldy mess. Then people said I had a nose for trouble.

Mostly my sense of smell is a good thing, though.

I was glad for it when I got to my new school and the bus driver lowered me on the electric platform to the sidewalk. After she drove away, I just sat there for a minute. If I concentrated, I could still smell Mom's shampoo clinging to my left shoulder, and Dad's shaving soap clinging to my right. I smiled to myself and gave my wheels a good, hard push. I started up the ramp.

A few kids ran up the steps and pushed in through the wide green doors. A burst of school smells hit my face. Those, at least, were the same as at my old school: chalk dust, pencil shavings, copier ink, and floor wax. I shut my eyes for a second and breathed deeply, pretending I was still at Fort Hill.

When I opened my eyes, the green doors were closing slowly. For a split second I saw the dark shape of a grown-up standing inside, just beyond the light. Whoever it was was wearing glasses and staring straight at me. It wasn't the staring that felt so strange. I'm used to being stared at when I go to new places. But this person suddenly jumped out of sight. When I got to the door and pushed it open, there was nobody there. Only a faint smell of wood smoke.

I pulled open the second set of doors and wheeled into the hallway. No grown-up in glasses there, either.

The principal was standing outside her office talking to a few kids. I'd met her the week before, when I'd visited with Mom and Dad. We had to make sure my wheelchair would fit through the doors and all. Lansford Elementary's an old school. It didn't even have a ramp till they heard I was coming. Ms. Kohlberg had said everything was ready for me. Or almost

everything. There was no ramp yet at the outside door to my classroom, but it would be built soon. Meanwhile, I'd just have to come around front at recess time.

"Hi, Ms. Kohlberg," I called.

"Hi, Maggie. Welcome!"

"Thanks!" I called back, but I kept on wheeling down the hall. She didn't follow me. She didn't make a big deal of me at all. I was starting to like Ms. Kohlberg.

I didn't remember the hall being so long. The fifth-grade room was way at the other end. Lots of kids were walking toward me. I looked straight at them and smiled. Some kids said "Hi" and smiled back. I knew a lot of them would turn around for a better look after they passed me. But they'd probably look hard at any new kid in the school. I used to do that when a new kid came to Fort Hill.

I was getting near my classroom. Suddenly, there was a sweet, damp smell. It was familiar, but I couldn't place it. Some smells I know right away: bacon, or popcorn; gasoline, or skunk. But other smells are more like memories. I have to let them come back slowly.

This smell just made me think of green.

5

When I got to the open doorway, I knew why. My classroom was a jungle of plants. They hadn't been there the other day.

I was one of the first few kids.

"Good morning," Mr. Buckley said when he saw me.

He was leaning down to water a real tree in a huge clay pot. He put the watering can down and came over to me. The other day, he'd been wearing sweatpants and an old sweatshirt. He looked taller and thinner in his tie and teacher clothes.

"Where would you like to sit?" he asked.

There weren't any kids' desks in Mr. Buckley's classroom. Just some big, round tables. I wheeled toward an empty one, and Mr. Buckley pulled a chair out of my way. I opened my saddlebag and set out my new notebook and a couple of pencils.

"Mind helping me water?" Mr. Buckley asked. He pointed to the window shelf, which was crammed full of plants. There was another watering can there. "Guess you didn't meet my plants the other day. I just brought them back. It's a big change for them. They're confused. So, talk to them, okay?"

The shelf was plenty low enough, and I was glad to be busy. Kids kept coming in, some through the outside door, some from the hall. They all knew each other, of course. They were talking and laughing, same as I would be if I were back at Fort Hill.

"Katie! Come sit here!"

"Hey! Some haircut, Mike! Your little brother give it to you?"

"Nice tan, Dee."

A bell rang. Mr. Buckley went to close the classroom door.

"Settle down now, please," he called out. "Sit anywhere, but only five to a table."

There were some groans and some shuffling around. I put the watering can down and wheeled back to my place. There were four other kids at my table: three girls and a real small, pale boy. The girl next to me had short, blondish hair like mine, but curly. Her shirt and jeans were brand-new. I could smell that new-clothes smell.

"Hi," I said, "I'm Maggie. I'm new." Then I kind of giggled and added, "In case you hadn't noticed."

The girls all kind of giggled, too. "My

name's Jo," said the blonde one, "spelled the girl's way. No 'e'.

"And this is Debby . . ."

Debby had her hair pulled back into one braid. She kind of ducked her head at me.

"And I'm Tina," the third girl said. She had little shells braided into her hair. They clicked as she nodded at me. "I was new last year," she said, and smiled as if she understood *exactly* how I felt.

I went over the names in my head to keep them straight: blonde Jo, shy Debby, friendly Tina.

I looked at the pale boy next to me. He folded his hands on the table and stared at his knuckles.

I looked at Jo. She turned her hands up and shrugged. She whispered as if he couldn't hear her, "He's new, too!"

I was about to ask the kid his name. Then I noticed something beyond him that made me get all self-conscious. A face with glasses was peering through the little window in the classroom door. It was staring straight at me. I saw it clearly before it jerked away out of sight.

Chapter 2

$\mathcal{M}$r. Buckley rummaged around on his desk at the back of the room.

"Attendance," he muttered. "Attendance."

I kept glancing at the door. I couldn't help it. Something was weird about that person with the glasses.

"I wonder where Dee got that tan," Tina was saying.

Jo was quick to answer. "Her dad won the lottery. They bought a castle in Spain."

Debby looked amazed. "Really? Why'd they come back here?"

"He bet all his money on the bullfights," Jo said. She was really good at keeping a straight face. "He went bankrupt."

"Really?" Debby said.

Tina groaned. "Come on, Deb. You'll believe anything!"

Jo just grinned.

I went over the names in my head again: Jo tells stories; Debby believes them; Tina keeps things real.

Then I glanced at the door again. No face. I started to relax.

Mr. Buckley found the right piece of paper. He grabbed a pencil and stood by the potted tree.

"Raise your hand, please, when I call your name . . .

". . . Josephine Abbott," he started.

Jo raised her hand. "But don't *ever* call me Josephine," she whispered to me.

"Joseph*ee-een!*" some guy called in a high, squeaky voice.

Jo gave him an angry look.

"That's Mark Lowman," she told me. "In the sweatshirt. He's a jerk."

Debby and Tina nodded.

"We can do without the comments, please," Mr. Buckley said.

But as he read the list, every name got some kind of reaction. "Hey!" someone would say, or "All *right!*" Or someone would wave from another table.

"Mark Lowman."

Mark grinned. The boys on either side of him lifted his arms by the wrists as if he were a hero.

"A real jerk," Jo muttered.

"Margaret Mitzkovitz," Mr. Buckley called out. He was looking right at me, but it took me a second to click: People who type up names always figure my name's a nickname. Once I got listed as Magdalene.

"Oh, *me,* you mean," I said to Mr. Buckley. "Except it's Maggie." Absolutely everybody was looking at me.

"Short for?" Mr. Buckley asked.

Mark Lowman leaned forward a little, still grinning.

"It's just Maggie," I said. "That's my real name."

"Okay, Maggie, thanks," said Mr. Buckley. "And welcome."

He scribbled on the paper as he called out the next few names. Debby was Deborah Smith. Tina was Christina Tinknell.

Mr. Buckley was writing on the paper again when he called the last name: "Cedrick Zinger."

Mark Lowman kind of snorted behind his hands. Otherwise there was silence. Everybody looked around, including me. The small kid next to me was still staring at his knuckles. His ears had turned bright red. The rest of his face was starting to match. He looked like he couldn't move. I leaned over and grabbed his wrist and raised his hand. He didn't look up or anything, but Mr. Buckley checked him off.

"Welcome, Cedrick."

"Just Rick," the kid mumbled.

"All here," said Mr. Buckley. "Great. Now let me clarify a few rules for this classroom." He started strolling around among the tables.

"No assigned seats. Sit anywhere you like." He stopped and looked straight at Mark Lowman. "Unless, of course, there's trouble." He started strolling again. "Respect one another. Respect me. And for that matter, respect the plants. Any questions?"

That's when the fire alarm went off. It was just as loud and angry as the one at Fort Hill. The pale kid next to me jumped up and made

for the outside door. Everybody else was just talking and laughing.

"Cedrick?" Mr. Buckley said. The kid stopped, looking embarrassed, but he didn't turn around. He kept his hand on the doorknob.

"Quiet, class!" Mr. Buckley called out. He was coming over to me. "Line up quickly and *quietly,* please!"

Everybody jumped up at once—except me, of course. They all left their chairs pushed out, right in my way.

"Sorry, Maggie," Mr. Buckley said. He was pulling chairs aside. "We didn't get a chance to rehearse this." He sounded really worried. That surprised me, and suddenly I felt worried, too. The alarm was still blaring. Lots of kids covered their ears. If I did that, I wouldn't be able to move.

I got into line behind Jo and Debby and Tina.

". . . a real fire, for sure," Jo was saying.

Debby's eyes widened.

"Come on, Jo, you're scaring her," Tina said.

Jo's grin was only half a grin. "Well, you've got to admit, it's pretty weird, a fire drill before we even have to do any work."

14

Mr. Buckley was leaning over his plants to close the windows. *"Slowly* now, class," he called out. "Cedrick, please hold the door. Now walk *slowly,* class, to the far end of the playground."

It wasn't till I got near the door that I remembered.

"Oops," I said. "No ramp."

Chapter 3

I started to turn my chair around.

Suddenly that small kid Cedrick was there in front of me. He looked scared—I mean *really* scared. His face was gray, and he was kind of shaky.

"No!" he said. He was whispering, but with the force of a yell.

"I can't go out *that* way," I said.

But when I started to move forward, Cedrick grabbed my wheelchair. He was leaning so close to me I could smell toothpaste. I could even see sweat on his face. He looked so weak I knew I could push right by him, but I stopped. It was spooky how scared the kid looked. I wished that alarm would quit blaring.

Then Mr. Buckley was there. "It's okay, Cedrick. I'll help Maggie." Mr. Buckley sounded really tense. "Go on out, Cedrick."

"Just Rick," I heard the kid mumble as he let go of my chair.

"Maggie," Mr. Buckley said firmly, "I'll have to carry you out. Just this once." He turned my chair back around.

"No!" I said. I forgot to be polite. I grabbed the wheels of my chair and pushed against Mr. Buckley. I hate being carried anyway. But in fifth grade? On the first day of school? With everyone—including a jerk like Mark Lowman—watching? And by a *teacher?* "No way!" I said.

Cedrick turned in the doorway and looked at me. I thought he was going to faint. Mr. Buckley stopped pushing me.

"Go on out, Cedrick," he said. "I'll help Maggie."

"Just Rick," Cedrick muttered. But he still stood there.

"Go on, Just Rick!" I said. "I'll race ya!"

Before Mr. Buckley even knew what happened, I turned my chair and wheeled for the door. Then I had to stop to open it. Mr. Buckley caught up to me.

"Maggie," he said, "I can't let you. It might be a real fire."

But he helped me with the door. The alarm was even louder in the empty hall. I took off for the front door. Mr. Buckley had to hurry to keep up.

"This is crazy," he said. He sounded out of breath.

Then we heard sirens, even over the blaring alarm. I pushed even faster. There was a sharp, nasty smell by the principal's office. I'd smelled it before, but I couldn't stop to think what it was.

Mr. Buckley held the doors, so I got out fast. There were two firefighters running up the ramp, a man and a woman. The man was just jamming his hat on over his bald head. The hat said CHIEF on the front.

"Cripes!" he said when he saw us. "Hurry! This is no drill!"

We went around to the side of the building. Firefighters were swarming toward every door. Finally the alarm stopped. We crossed to the

edge of the hardtop. Then there was bumpy grass, so I had to let Mr. Buckley push me. It was so crowded and noisy, nobody noticed anyway.

Except Cedrick. He came up to me and looked at the ground.

"Hi, Just Rick," I said.

"Beat ya," he said.

I laughed. "Yeah," I said, "but *you* took the shortcut!"

He grinned at the ground. Mr. Buckley had moved away, calling, "Fifth grade! Over here!"

"Why were you so scared?" I asked Just Rick.

His grin disappeared. He kicked at the grass with one foot.

"Sorry," I said. "None of my business."

He glanced up at me, then looked down again. "That's okay," he said to the ground. "It's just . . ."

Jo came hurrying over with Debby and Tina.

"Did you see anything?" Jo asked. "Smoke? Flames?"

As I shook my head, Cedrick walked away.

"Maybe we'll get to go home!" Tina said.

Jo giggled. "Great way to get out of school," she said. "Set a fire on the first day."

"*Set* it!" Debby said. "Somebody *set* it?"

"Come on, Debby!" Tina said.

Jo grinned. "You never know," she said. "Someday one of my stories might come true."

"Well," I said, "*I* didn't see anything." Then I remembered. "I did *smell* something, but I'm not sure what."

The girls didn't seem very interested. They were watching some firefighters coming out of the school. Ms. Kohlberg stepped out of the crowd and went to talk to them.

I closed my eyes for a second, trying to remember the smell. It wouldn't come back to me. Instead, my mind kept making a picture of clowns. Then another smell—very faint—blew from behind me on the breeze. Wood smoke. I opened my eyes and twisted in my chair to look around. The face with the glasses was just ducking behind a bunch of sixth-graders. This time, I could tell it was a woman.

"Jo," I said, "who's that woman over there? With the glasses."

"I don't see anyone with glasses."

"Can you go look for me? She's wearing blue."

I could see Jo thought I was weird, but she just shrugged.

"Sure," she said.

Debby and Tina went with her. They came back in a couple of minutes.

"Blue sweater?" Jo asked. "Really short hair? Glasses?"

"Yeah. Who is she?"

"I think she's an alien who's . . ."

"Come on, Jo," I said.

"Well, actually, she's a spy from . . ."

"Jo!" Tina said.

Even Debby giggled.

Jo grinned.

"Okay," she said. "I'll tell the truth." She raised one hand like a witness in court. "I know everyone in this school. Blue Sweater's a stranger. Never saw her before in my life."

Chapter 4

*T*he regular bell rang. We could go back into the building.

"Shucks," said Tina. "No day off."

"Line up, class!" Mr. Buckley called out. "False alarm."

"That's what he thinks," Jo said. "Until the mad firebug strikes again!"

"Firebug?" said Debby.

"Debby!" Tina said with a groan, and Jo giggled.

"See ya," I said. "I have to go around front."

"We'll go that way, too," Jo said. "I bet he won't care."

She started striding toward the hardtop. Debby and Tina followed. I pushed really hard, but one wheel was in a little rut. I couldn't even turn my chair. I felt like yelling at the girls.

"Oops!" Jo said. She turned back toward me. "Sorry."

"That's okay," I said, because suddenly it was. "I just need a push over the rough parts."

Jo pushed. Debby and Tina walked beside me. They didn't have much to say all of a sudden.

"Oh, Jose*phee-een!*" I already recognized that voice. Mark Lowman was at the end of the line that was following Mr. Buckley back to our classroom. "Jose*phee-een,*" he called again. "You look real cute as a nurse, Josephine!"

"Jerk," Jo muttered over my shoulder.

"Double jerk," I said.

We got to the hardtop. I sat up extra tall. I wheeled myself along with extra dignity. I knew Mark Lowman wouldn't notice or care, but at least it made me feel better. I'd have to get back at Mark Lowman some other way.

When we passed by the principal's office, I couldn't smell whatever it was anymore. There were some teachers and kids milling around.

The fire chief was talking to Ms. Kohlberg. She glanced at me as I passed.

"Could I speak to you for a minute, please, Maggie?"

I'd been looking forward to going up the hall with the other kids, but you don't say "No" to the principal.

"See you in a minute," I said to Jo and Debby and Tina.

I watched them swing along toward our room.

The fire chief was just leaving.

"We haven't got a clue," he was saying to Ms. Kohlberg. "Could've just been a spider in a smoke detector. But keep an eye out. I can't tell you what to look for. Anything unusual." He sighed. *"Anything."*

"Thank you, Mr. Gibb."

The fire chief left, and Ms. Kohlberg turned to me. "Come on in, Maggie."

I fit through the first door okay—into the secretary's office. But there was a second door into where Ms. Kohlberg's desk was. A huge copy machine was jammed into the corner behind the secretary's desk. It hadn't been there when I visited before. Now the second door wouldn't open all the way.

"Oh, dear," said Ms. Kohlberg. She leaned against the copier and pushed with all her weight. "This monster may be more trouble than it's worth."

"I think I can make it," I said.

I had to be careful my knuckles didn't stick out beyond the wheels, but I slid through.

Ms. Kohlberg closed the door behind me.

"Needless to say, Maggie," she began, "we didn't plan this false alarm." She sat down at her desk and turned sideways to face me. "But I learned something."

I stared at all the papers on her desk. There were four neat piles with labels on top: TO READ. TO COPY. TODAY! SOMEDAY?

"The ramp from your classroom was supposed to be built this weekend," Ms. Kohlberg went on. "We thought that would be soon enough."

I nodded without looking at her.

"But it isn't soon enough, Maggie. The fire chief's going to speed things up. Maybe we can get a crew busy tomorrow."

I still wasn't sure what her point was.

"Right now, this school isn't safe for you, Maggie."

I looked straight at her, and she kept going.

"What you did was very dangerous. If that had been a real fire . . ."

"I *hate* being carried," I said.

"I understand, Maggie. It's not your fault. You shouldn't have to choose. It's the school's job—*my* job—to be sure every student is safe."

"I'm okay," I said.

"Thank heaven," she said with a big sigh. She seemed to be talking to herself. Then she looked at me again.

"But I'm afraid, Maggie . . ." She paused and I looked away. "I'm afraid we're going to have to send you home until that ramp is built."

I knew if I said anything, I would scream at her. *Are you* kidding! *Send me* home? *On the first day of school? Why do you have to make a big deal of me? Why do you have to treat me differently? I'm different enough!*

I kept my eyes down. I squeezed both arms of my wheelchair with all my anger.

"I'm sorry, Maggie. I know this is very unfair."

"There's not even anyone there," I said. "Mom and Dad are both at work."

"I know. I'll have to call them. It will take

28

some arranging. You'll be here at least for the morning. But the fire chief insists, and I have to agree. We can't take the risk.''

I really wanted to yell at her. *It's* my *risk. Why can't* I *decide?* I just kept reminding myself she was the principal. You don't yell at principals.

I had to go very slowly through the door by the copier. I had to go very slowly among the people still milling around. When I got to the hall, I went faster. I wanted to speed. I wanted to wheel as fast as I could, on and on, until I got too tired to be angry anymore.

I passed the door with the little blue sign of a person in a wheelchair: another way I was different. Other girls used the girls' room and giggled in there together. But the girls' room was over behind the stage, and there were two steps up to that hallway. I was stuck being the only kid using a teachers' bathroom.

I stopped. At least I could be alone in there. I backed up and went in. I sat at the sink and looked in the mirror.

Just seeing my upper body, I looked pretty normal—except for having thicker arms. Most fifth-graders don't lift weights. Most fifth-graders don't have a physical therapist who visits twice a week. Mine gets me out of my chair to do push-ups.

Suddenly I was crying. I turned the water on and let it run.

"Tina *wanted* the day off," I said aloud. "Why couldn't they send *her* home?"

Then I splashed my face with water and dried it with a paper towel. I figured I'd better get back to class.

The lock on the door stuck. For a second, I thought I was going to have to yell to get out of there. But then the lock turned free.

Chapter 5

*M*r. Buckley was trying to teach a math les-
son. My place at the table was cleared
free of chairs, and there was a textbook waiting
for me. Someone had opened it to the right
page. The book smelled new—all sharp and
glossy.

As I got settled, Jo whispered, "What'd she
say?"

"They're going to build the ramp sooner," I
whispered back.

I didn't say anything about going home.
Maybe Ms. Kohlberg wouldn't reach Mom or
Dad. Maybe it wouldn't work out.

"Just try the problems on page 17," Mr.

Buckley was saying. He picked a few dead leaves off a plant. "They might be too hard or too easy, or just hard enough. That's what I need to know."

They were just hard enough for me. I could do them, but I had to think. I made some mistakes. Math time always smells like erasers to me. While I was thinking, I glanced at Just Rick. He was done already.

"Are you a math whiz?" I whispered.

He shrugged and looked down at his paper. I took that for a "yes."

I still wondered what had scared him so. Maybe he'd tell me at lunch. I could already smell what lunch was going to be: pizza. And something chocolate for dessert.

I was right about the food, but not about Just Rick. At lunch, he sat way down at the end of the room, all by himself. I had my tray in my lap and was thinking about wheeling down there, but I'd have to pass Mark Lowman. Mark Lowman was getting kids to arm-wrestle with him. If he won, he got their chocolate cake. He already had a big stack of it on his tray.

Then Jo came up beside me.

"Did Ms. Kohlberg tell you anything about the fire?"

"No, but I heard the fire chief talk about clues."

"Clues? Ooo!"

Debby and Tina came up. We all sat together.

Jo was all excited about what Mr. Gibb had said. " 'Anything unusual.' See! He means strangers! I *told* you it's a mad firebug!"

"Come on, Jo," Tina said. "Debby's getting too scared to eat."

Jo paid no attention. "Only strange person around here," she said, "is that lady of yours, Maggie—the one with the glasses."

"Yeah," I said. "She's strange all right. I keep seeing her. And smelling her."

"*Smelling* her!" Debby said, looking a little sick.

"Yeah," I said, "I'm weird that way." I explained to them about my sense of smell.

Jo seemed really interested. "So what does Blue Sweater smell like?"

"Wood smoke," I said. "Kind of a nice smell. We had a wood stove where I used to live. I got so I could tell if we were burning oak or maple."

"See!" said Jo. "Smoke! Blue Sweater's the firebug!"

Debby started looking around the lunchroom. She poked at her pizza and looked around again. She seemed kind of pale.

I felt a little spooked, too. I knew Jo just liked wild stories, but that wood-smoke woman *was* pretty strange. I laughed a little to make myself feel better.

"Okay," I said to Jo. "So why's a mad arsonist watching *me* all the time?"

Jo didn't even stop to think. "She's also a mad kidnapper. She's trying to trap you alone. Then she'll grab you!"

"Why?" Debby asked, really serious.

"Debby," Tina moaned.

"Ransom!" Jo went on. "Maggie's got rich parents." She turned to me. "Right?"

I shook my head and smiled. "Sorry. Dad's a builder, and the reason we moved here is he's going to business school. And right now, Mom's a bank teller—part-time." This was getting to be fun, making Jo work things into her story.

"Aha!" she said. "The bank! Blue Sweater wants ransom from the bank!"

I laughed. "And she has a getaway van with a wheelchair lift, right?"

"How do you know?" Debby asked.

The rest of us burst out laughing.

Debby laughed, too. "Okay," she said, "you got me again." She started eating her pizza.

"Hey," said Tina. "That Zinger kid's new."

"And strange," said Debby.

"That's just 'cause he's smart," I said. "Smart people are different."

"But Deb's right," Jo said. She glanced over her shoulder. "He was acting awful strange when the fire bell rang."

I remembered how scared he'd looked—*really* scared. But he'd tried to help me anyway.

"Maybe *he's* the firebug," Jo said. "Maybe . . ."

"Anybody want my chocolate cake?" I asked. I didn't want to hear a Jo story about Just Rick just now.

"Don't you want it?" Tina asked.

"Too much baking soda," I said.

"But you haven't tasted it," Debby said.

"I can smell it."

"I'm not *that* gullible," Debby said proudly. She took a big bite of her cake. Her face went sour, and she swallowed hard. "Yuck," she said. "You're right. Too much of *something,* anyway."

Jo had been thinking. "I know. That little smart kid got kicked out of his old school. Too many fires in the boys' room, so . . ."

I tried to think of something else to talk about. But I didn't have to. In the middle of Jo's sentence, the fire alarm went off.

Chapter 6

Jo jumped up.

"I told you!" she said. She tried to grin, but she looked a little worried, as if she was starting to believe her own stories.

Debby looked terrified. "Let's get out of here," she said.

"Yeah," Tina said, and they all three headed for the door.

"Hey!" I called, but the alarm was too loud.

The teacher on duty was clapping her hands and yelling for quiet. No one seemed to care. Some kids were still eating. Some were clearing their trays. Some were just standing around, joking and laughing. I guess everyone figured it was a false alarm again. I wasn't so sure. I wanted to get out of there.

At least the lunchroom was closer to the front door. But it also had more chairs in it. I turned from side to side, using the footrests to shove chairs away. Wobbling like that slowed me down. Then I heard a familiar voice, all squeaky and fake.

"Oh, look!"

I'd steered right toward Mark Lowman and his buddies.

"Well, if it isn't Josephine's cripple!"

"Excuse me," I said very firmly, and just tried to push on through.

"Don't worry," Mark Lowman said. He made his voice all gooey. "I'll help."

He grabbed the back handles of my wheelchair and pushed. I pushed backward against him.

"Let go!" I demanded.

A couple of his friends snickered.

"Just call me Josephine," Mark squeaked.

"Quiet!"

The teacher on duty was standing on a chair now. Everybody heard her this time.

Mark let go, and I took off. At least he'd gotten me closer to the door. I'd get him back later. Somehow.

A whole bunch of teachers appeared in the doorway. They must have all been in the teachers' room. They spread out and started telling kids what to do. Mr. Buckley came up to me.

"Here we go again, Maggie," he said. He smiled, but he looked old or something. "Lead the way!"

We were almost down the ramp when the firefighters got there. The chief gave Mr. Buckley a sharp look, as if to ask, *Why's* she *still here?* I sat up straighter and pushed faster.

Jo came running up when we were halfway across the hardtop.

"Sorry," she said to me. "I just forgot. I mean, you don't seem . . . I mean, you seem so . . ."

"That's okay," I said.

"You all set?" Mr. Buckley asked me. "I've got to get a head count." I nodded and he ran ahead. He held up his hand and shouted, "Fifth grade! Fifth grade over here!"

Jo leaned down as if telling a secret. "I told you that Zinger kid was strange. He's still in there somewhere. Probably covering up the evidence."

I wheeled my chair around and headed back for the ramp. I was moving faster than I thought I ever could. The alarm was still screaming.

"Just Rick?" I called, as if anyone could hear me.

The ramp slowed me down. Jo stood at the bottom and hollered at me. I couldn't hear what she was saying. Then the alarm bell stopped.

"Come back, Maggie," Jo was shouting. "You're crazy!"

I got all the way to the principal's office. Then the woman firefighter saw me.

"Whoa!" she said, grabbing my chair. "Where do you think you're going?"

"There's a kid in here. A short guy."

"We found him," she said. She was turning my chair around. I smelled something. A memory flashed in my head. Or a dream. A feeling of being off the ground. But I was listening to the firefighter.

"He's okay," she went on. "Just terrified. Wouldn't leave. We had to carry him."

I let her wheel me out. I was *very* tired all of a sudden.

"Why?" I asked. We were on the ramp. I took a deep breath of fresh air.

"Said he was looking for someone," the firefighter answered. "A friend who uses a wheelchair. He thought she might be trapped."

I craned my neck to look back at her. "Oh, no," I said.

The woman kind of laughed. "I can see he didn't need to worry about *you!*" she said. "He's in a lot worse shape than you are!"

Jo came running up.

"You scared me, Maggie!" she said. She sounded angry.

"Sorry," was all I could say.

Jo walked with us across the hardtop.

"Where's the fire?" she asked.

"We're still checking," the firefighter said. "Could be another false alarm."

I bounced a bit as she pushed my chair onto the grass, right toward a bunch of teachers and a couple of firefighters. Some were standing and some were crouched down. There was a kid lying on the ground. A firefighter's coat was spread over him like a blanket.

"What's your name?" a firefighter asked.

"His name's Cedrick," Mr. Buckley answered.

I was close enough now to see the pale, scared face.

"No," I said firmly. "That's Just Rick."

A little smile crossed his face. I saw it.

Chapter 7

When the bell rang for us to go inside, they took Just Rick to the nurse's office.

"Don't worry," Mr. Buckley told me. "He just needs some peace and quiet. He had a bad fright."

"Can I stop in and say hi?" I asked. "I have to go in that way anyway."

"Sure," he said. Then he raised his voice. "Come on, fifth grade. Back to class. It's writing time. We might even get some work done."

Kids groaned and laughed.

"Hey," I heard Mark Lowman say, "I never got to eat my chocolate cake."

I wished they'd *make* him eat it. The whole

stack. And mine, too. That chocolate cake was about what he deserved.

I was afraid Ms. Kohlberg would call me aside again, but she and the fire chief were talking. I slowed down and listened.

"Still no clue," he said. "Could be a faulty smoke detector." He sighed as if he was awfully tired. "Or a spider that hides when we get here. But we haven't found anything."

Ms. Kohlberg spoke very low. All I heard was ". . . someone . . . trouble . . . for some reason?"

"Could be," Mr. Gibb answered. I kept going. I didn't want them to notice me. Maybe they'd forget about sending me home.

Just Rick was alone in the nurse's office. He was propped up on the cot. He looked a lot better already.

"Hi," he said.

"You okay?" I asked.

"Yeah."

"Thanks, by the way," I said.

"Sure."

"You get real scared," I said.

"Yeah." He looked at his hands for a second.

Then he went on. "Our house burned down. That's why we moved here."

Now I was the one looking at my hands.

"Everyone okay?" I asked. Then I was afraid to hear the answer.

"Yeah," he said. "In the end."

"Good," I said.

"But it was awful," he said.

"I bet."

He was quiet again. He glanced at my skinny legs.

"What about you?" he asked.

I knew what he was asking about. "A problem with my spine," I answered. "When I was born. I've never been any different." Then I laughed. "I mean, I've *always* been different. I'm used to it."

He smiled.

"But sometimes," I added, "I wish I could be different—I mean, *not* different."

"I bet."

We were both quiet for a minute.

"Are you coming back to class?" I asked.

Just Rick nodded.

"Are you smart in writing, too?"

He shrugged.

"Social studies?"

He shrugged again.

"So you're different, too," I said.

He smiled a little, but shrugged again. I figured he'd wear his shoulders out if I didn't quit asking him questions.

"See ya," I said.

I practically had to bump into him to turn around.

"See ya," he said, when I couldn't see him anymore.

I stopped in at the bathroom. I was thinking about what a weird day it was turning out to be. Even if I had to leave now, it wouldn't be *so* bad. I didn't exactly feel new anymore. Just Rick had told that firefighter he was looking for a friend.

When I was washing my hands, I looked in the mirror and smiled at myself.

There was one of those bottles of liquid soap. It smelled like lilacs. I used a lot of it.

Maybe Jo would be a friend, too, I thought. What a wild imagination she had!

Then the fire alarm went off again.

"Stupid spider!" I said aloud.

I reached for the lock.

It stuck. My soapy hands just slid around.

I took a deep breath and tried again. My hands were too slippery.

"Help!" I yelled, but I could hardly even hear myself over the alarm. I kept telling myself it was no big deal. Some spider in a smoke detector. But I was scared. And getting more scared. What if Jo was right? What if someone was doing this on purpose? Even the chief had said it was possible. What if this time there really was a fire?

The brown paper towels were stacked on the sink. When I grabbed one, the whole pile spilled over onto the floor. I dried my hands and just dropped the towel. I tried the lock again.

Now the *lock* was all slippery.

I heard some people running by. I pounded on the door.

"Help!"

The footsteps faded.

I turned my chair to try to reach some towels on the floor.

There were no more footsteps. Everyone must be outside by now. Even Just Rick. He wouldn't be so foolish again.

I got a towel and swiped at the lock.

The smell of wet brown paper was getting thick. It felt hard to breathe. I wished Ms. Kohlberg *had* sent me home.

I tried the lock again.

It turned.

The door opened before I could grab the handle.

There was a smell of wood smoke.

I looked up.

Short hair. Glasses. Blue sweater.

"Hello, Maggie," she said. "I've been looking for you."

Chapter 8

Jo was right. This weird woman *was* after me!

I started to back up—as if I had anywhere to back to.

"Come with me," Blue Sweater said. "Quick." She stood aside, holding the door open with her back.

My heart was jumping so much, I tried to swallow to keep it down, but my mouth had gone dry.

I wheeled out. I had no choice.

I pretended to be calm. I turned my chair slowly toward the front door.

Then I took off.

Blue Sweater ran after me and got ahead to the door. She stood with her back to it.

I pushed harder. I figured I'd just ram through. It worked. She jumped backwards and pushed the door open just as I got to it.

"What the . . . ?" she said.

The second set of doors opened in. I had to stop and deal with them. Blue Sweater caught her balance and came over. She leaned over me, trying to get the door handle before I did. I shoved her away. All those push-ups paid off. She kind of fell back against the wall.

"Hey!" she said.

I was out on the ramp before she could catch up. I wheeled down fast. Too fast. I scared myself. But I got down and around the corner of the building onto the hardtop. It was like a carnival out there—kids running and shouting and tossing Frisbees.

Mr. Buckley came running over, and Just Rick, and Jo. I was really glad to see them.

"You were right, Jo," I said. I was all out of breath.

Everyone spoke at once: "About what?" Jo asked. "You okay?" Just Rick asked. "Where were you?" Mr. Buckley asked.

"Blue Sweater. Fine. The bathroom," I puffed.

"Thank heaven she found you," Mr. Buckley said.

"Who?" I asked.

Mr. Buckley didn't even answer. I couldn't believe what he did. He sat down—right on the hardtop. He put his knees up and leaned on them. "If I live through this day . . ." he said.

I heard footsteps running up behind me. Mr. Buckley stood up again.

"I see you've met Ms. Dalrymple," he said.

"Ms. Who?"

Blue Sweater came up in front of me and put out her hand. "Hannah Dalrymple," she said. "Pleased to meet you." She looked at Mr. Buckley, then back at me. "I'd hardly call this girl disabled," she said. "She nearly ran me over. Then she almost knocked me down! I'm not sure she qualifies for my services!"

"Who *are* you?" I demanded. I was too confused to be polite.

Mr. Buckley laughed. "Ms. Dalrymple is the special-education coordinator for the district," he said.

"Just a disguise!" I heard Jo whisper.

"I came to observe your first day," Blue Sweater, or rather Ms. Dalrymple, explained. She was smiling now. "Ms. Kohlberg said you hate being singled out. I've been, shall we say, in hiding. But when this last alarm rang, I offered to go find you."

"Excuse me," Jo said to her, "but I just need to check something out. Do you by any chance heat with wood?"

Ms. Dalrymple looked as confused as I was feeling. "Wood?" she said. "You mean at home? We have an old wood stove, if that's what you mean. Smoky old thing. Why?"

Jo grinned. She leaned over and whispered right in my ear. "The nose knows!" Then she sauntered off toward the rest of the fifth grade. The alarm stopped.

"Come on, Rick," Mr. Buckley said. He gave a big, loud sigh. "Let's leave these two to get acquainted."

Just Rick waved by lifting his arm from the elbow and letting it flop again. They walked off.

I was left facing the short hair and glasses again.

"Sorry," I said. "I'd seen you watching me.

I thought . . ." Now it seemed too silly to explain.

"You had a big scare, getting trapped like that."

I looked beyond her at the field. It was like an all-school recess. Kids were running all over the place. The first grade was playing "Duck, Duck, Goose." No one seemed worried anymore.

"Just another false alarm," I said.

"Yeah," she said. "But until we know it's false, we still get alarmed."

I saw the fire chief come out and speak to Ms. Kohlberg. Then he went back in again.

"So how's your first day going?" Ms. Dalrymple asked. Then she laughed. "Forget I asked that," she said. "This has got to be the craziest first day anyone ever had anywhere. It's been more like a circus than a school!"

A circus. My mind made that picture of clowns again. Suddenly I could smell something that wasn't even there. It was the memory of a smell—sharp and clear and nasty.

"Excuse me," I said. I started wheeling toward Ms. Kohlberg.

"Can I help?" Ms. Dalrymple called.

"No thanks," I called back.

Ms. Kohlberg saw me coming and came toward me.

"Oh, Maggie," she said. "I still haven't reached your parents. Our lines were busy and then . . ."

"I know what it is!" I interrupted. "I know what the problem is!"

Chapter 9

I told Ms. Kohlberg my idea. She asked a teacher to take charge while she was gone. Then she marched right along beside me as we went around front and into the building again.

"Mr. Gibb!" she called as we got inside. Her voice echoed down the empty hall. "Mr. Gibb?"

The woman firefighter appeared from the lunchroom. "I'll get him," she said.

The smell was still there in the hallway. Very faint, but just as I remembered it.

We went into the secretary's office. The smell was a little stronger.

"Now can you smell it?" I asked Ms. Kohlberg.

She sniffed and shook her head.

"Smell what?" It was the fire chief in the doorway. His hat was off. His bald head was smudged with dirt. He looked very tired.

"Maggie here has a theory," Ms. Kohlberg said. She had me tell Mr. Gibb.

"Could be," he said. "Shall we test it?"

Ms. Kohlberg took a blank piece of paper from the secretary's desk. She wrote CAUSE FOR ALARM in big letters.

"Would you like to do the honors, Ms. Mitzkovitz?"

She handed the paper to me.

I lifted the lid of the copier and put the paper in. I pushed the big green button that was just around my eye level. The copier hummed and the copy came out: CAUSE FOR ALARM. Nothing else happened.

"Guess not," I said.

"Try fifty copies," Mr. Gibb said.

Ms. Kohlberg leaned over and pushed some other buttons.

I pushed the green one again. Copies came rolling out. CAUSE FOR ALARM. CAUSE FOR ALARM. CAUSE FOR ALARM. The copier kept count in a little display window: 04 . . . 05 . . . 06. We were

all silent and still. The copies piled up: 37 . . .
38 . . . 39.

The smell was coming back—not a smoke
smell, but hot, nasty, sharp. Like that time Mom
and Dad took me to the circus. They were just
lowering me out of the van. Then the lift shorted
out. Some wires burned. I was stuck in midair,
staring at a poster of clowns. Mom grabbed the
fire extinguisher. Dad grabbed the hand crank.
They got me down. We even went to the circus.

The smell from the copier was really strong.
On the forty-sixth copy, the fire alarm went off.

"Cripes!" said Mr. Gibb. "You were right!"

"We just got this monster," Ms. Kohlberg
said. "It was supposed to be a big *help!*"

The firewoman and another guy came running in.

"No cause for alarm," Mr. Gibbs said, laughing. "Turn that thing off, would you. We've
heard it enough for one day!"

A minute later, the alarm stopped. We all
smiled.

I rolled away from the copier. Together, Ms.
Kohlberg and Mr. Gibb pushed and shoved it
out from the wall. Mr. Gibb leaned down to
unplug it, but he jerked his arm back.

"Cripes! That *is* hot." He glanced at me. "But *I* sure can't smell anything! Let's just wait a minute."

We all did.

When Mr. Gibb finally unplugged the copier, he held the plug up like a trophy.

"Amen," he said.

The other two firefighters stood in the doorway and clapped.

"Now," said Ms. Kohlberg. "Before we let everyone back in again. Please. I want two minutes with no sirens, no bells. Come sit down in my office and *explain* all this."

The door could swing wider now. She held it open and turned to me.

"Ms. Mitzkovitz," she said. She swept the air grandly with her arm. "Please lead the way."

I wheeled into her office. Everyone else came, too. The four neat piles were still on Ms. Kohlberg's desk. They were all about the same as before. Except the one labeled TODAY! That one was a whole lot bigger.

"So it was just a short circuit?" Ms. Kohlberg said.

She plopped down at her desk. Mr. Gibb sat in a nearby chair. The others sat on the couch.

"Well, actually," Mr. Gibb said, "it's nowhere near that simple. If it were just a short circuit...," He paused and smiled at me. "Well, I like to *think,* anyway, we could have found a short circuit without our olfactory detective here."

Ms. Kohlberg leaned toward me. "Olfactory refers to the sense of smell," she said.

I smiled. "I know," I said. "It's come up before."

"Usually," Mr. Gibb went on, "a short circuit causes a fire, and the fire sets off the alarm. But this time there was no fire. Not even a little smoke. Not a clue." Then he laughed. "For *normal* noses, anyway!"

We all laughed.

"In new schools," he went on, "the alarm system has its own circuit—its own set of wires. This is an old school. The copier was using the same wires as the fire alarm. Once that machine heated up a bit, it was drawing *lots* of electricity. That meant low voltage to the rest of the circuit. Any change in voltage triggers the relay switch on the alarm. What Maggie here smelled was hot plastic—the insulation and the plug. But before things got *too* hot, low voltage set off the alarm. Your secretary stopped copying and left. The wires cooled down and there was no fire."

Ms. Kohlberg looked worried. "You mean if we'd plugged that copier in on a different circuit, we might have had a real fire?"

"I'm afraid so."

"Then the alarm really *did* save us," Ms. Kohlberg said.

"The alarm and this young lady's nose for trouble!" Mr. Gibb concluded.

This was getting embarrassing. I didn't understand about circuits and voltage. All I'd done was recognize a smell.

"We'll have to get an electrician in here right away," said Ms. Kohlberg.

"And a ramp," Mr. Gibb added. "There's a temporary kind. Metal. We'll get one in by tomorrow. I'm not sure the school's safe without Ms. Mitzkovitz here."

I smiled, but I looked at my hands.

"You're okay for the rest of today," Mr. Gibb said to Ms. Kohlberg.

"The busses come in an hour anyway," Ms. Kohlberg said.

She stood up. "Let's ring the bell. But I'm declaring a holiday. Free time till the busses come. We'll start all over tomorrow. *Tomorrow* will be the first day of school!"

Chapter 10

Ms. Kohlberg wasn't kidding about the free time. Some classes watched videos in their rooms. A few classes stayed outside. Mr. Buckley got out puzzles and board games. Then he puttered with his plants.

Mark Lowman started another arm-wrestling contest. A bunch of his friends sat around cheering. He made each person bet something. He'd already won three erasers, two pencils, and a pair of bright-orange shoelaces.

I was playing Parcheesi with Just Rick and Jo and Tina. Debby was watching. I started to tell them about the copier.

"Oh!" Just Rick said, sounding excited all

of a sudden. "Overloaded circuit, right? I bet low voltage was what tripped the alarm."

I stopped shaking the dice. We were all looking at him. "How'd you know that?" I asked.

His ears were getting red. I guess he'd just forgotten himself for a second.

I rolled the dice and made a big deal about getting doubles, so everyone paid attention to me.

During Tina's turn, I whispered to Just Rick, *"Vive la différence!"* I figured I'd have to explain my French, but Just Rick smiled as if he understood. I was beginning to wonder if the kid knew everything.

Mr. Buckley announced that he'd be in the office for a minute. "Responsible behavior, please," he said. "I'll be right back." Then he left.

"Jose*phee-een!*"

We kept playing Parcheesi. Nobody turned to look at Mark Lowman.

"It's Nurse Josephine! Playing in the weirdo ward!"

Jo shook the dice in the little cardboard tube. She shook hard. She moved her little green disk four spaces. *Plunk. Plunk. Plunk. Plunk.*

It was my turn. I put down my little cardboard shaker.

"Excuse me," I said. "Take my place, Debby, okay?"

They didn't ask where I was going. They probably figured the bathroom.

I wheeled over to Mark Lowman's table.

"Next," he was saying.

The kid who'd just lost handed over his pencil sharpener, then stood up and moved away. I caught the empty chair with my footrest. I turned sharply to push the chair aside.

"I'm next," I said.

Mark Lowman grinned. "You gotta bet something."

"If you win," I said, "you get to keep being a jerk."

"Oooo!" said Mark's friends. Then: "Yeah!" and "All right!" They slapped him on the back.

"If I win," I said, "you have to keep all your stupid names and put-downs to yourself. Forever."

"Oooo!" "Yeah!" "All right!"

Mark's grin just got wider.

"It's a deal," he said.

He put out his hand and we shook. His grasp was really strong. Maybe I was making a big mistake.

I had to adjust my chair a few times to get the angle right. Mark watched and grinned. I put the brakes on.

No one was doing puzzles anymore. No one was playing Parcheesi. Everyone had crowded around us.

Mark and I locked hands. He looked surprised for a second. He'd expected a weakling. At least I'd make him think twice.

Our hands stayed straight up for a long time. Mark stopped grinning. His face scrunched up. His friends got very quiet.

"Go, Maggie!" Jo called.

Mark pushed harder. I couldn't hold him. My hand started to sink toward the table.

"No problem!" his friends cheered. "Take her right out, Marko!"

"Come on, Maggie," I heard. "Go, Maggie!" Lots of kids were cheering for me now. Not just Jo and Tina and Debby. Kids I hadn't even met yet.

I pushed our hands to straight-up again. My

shoulder was starting to hurt. My tongue, too, because I was biting it.

"Vive la différence!" a little voice cheered. Just Rick.

Mark sneered. He pushed out the words "Bunch of weirdos!"

That's when I flattened him. I just smacked his arm right down to the table. He twisted in his chair.

There was a split second of silence.

"Oooo!" a friend of Mark's moaned quietly.

Then the clapping erupted. It sounded like the whole class was clapping.

I leaned close to Mark Lowman.

"Remember the deal," I said.

Then I smiled at Just Rick. "Let's finish that Parcheesi," I said.

I undid the brakes and started turning around. Mr. Buckley was standing in the doorway. He was leaning against the jamb as if he'd been there for a while. He was smiling. The minute I saw him, he got all serious. He came into the room.

"What's going on here?" he asked sternly. "Back to your tables, class. Now!"

About an hour later, the special bus pulled up

in front of my house. The lift lowered me to the sidewalk. My little brother, Howie, ran out to greet me. He smelled like preschool—poster paint, mostly, and peanut butter.

Mom came out behind him.

"So how was Lansford Elementary?" she asked.

I grinned, trying to think of a word.

"Different," I said. "Really different."

I wheeled up the walk to our house. Howie ran beside me.

"Veeva lahdee French!" he said, and I had to agree with him.